SUGAR BAG BABY

ORCHARD BOOKS
96 Leonard Street, London EC2A 4XD
Orchard Books Australia
32/45-51 Huntley Street, Alexandria, NSW 2015
ISBN 1 84362 070 7 (hardback)
ISBN 1 84362 071 5 (paperback)
First published in Great Britain in 2003
First paperback publication in 2004
Text © Susan Gates 2003
Illustrations © Sebastien Braun 2003
The rights of Susan Gates to be identified as the author
and of Sebastien Braun to be identified as the illustrator of this
work have been asserted by them in accordance with the
Copyright, Designs and Patents Act, 1988.
A CIP catalogue record for this book is available
from the British Library.
1 3 5 7 9 10 8 6 4 2 (hardback)
1 3 5 7 9 10 8 6 4 2 (paperback)
Printed in Great Britain

SUGAR BAG BABY

SUSAN GATES
Illustrated by Sebastien Braun

ORCHARD BOOKS

CHAPTER 1

"Here we go again!" thought Sugar Bag Baby.

He should have been down at the Skate Park with his mates. But instead he was on the platform with the VIP's at the Village Fundraising Fête. He was the star of the show.

"The same old thing every year!" thought Sugar Bag Baby, sighing.

Everything about it made him cringe. Especially the huge, blow-up photo of himself that he was sitting beside. His mum lent it to the Fête every year.

"How could she?" thought Sugar Bag Baby. She knew it made him squirm with embarrassment.

It showed him in his incubator at two days old. He wasn't a pretty sight. He was on his back like a cockroach. His arms and legs looked like cocktail sticks. His tiny grey body was as wrinkly as a naked mole rat. But the worst thing was, he was wearing fluffy white mittens and bootees and a girly bonnet with ribbons that tied in a bow under his chin.

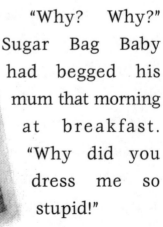

"Why? Why?" Sugar Bag Baby had begged his mum that morning at breakfast. "Why did you dress me so stupid!"

"You look cute!" Mum had protested. "Besides, premature babies have to be warm. And especially you. You were so teeny! You weighed less than a bag of sugar."

Sugar Bag Baby had groaned. He'd heard all this before.

"The whole village rallied round," Mum was telling him. "They were wonderful. They collected money to buy you that special incubator. Some pensioners gave their last one pee! You should be—"

"I know! I know!" Sugar Bag Baby had interrupted her. "I know I should be grateful. I know I'd probably be DEAD if it wasn't for them! You don't have to keep on reminding me! You don't have to keep on dragging me along to fundraising things!"

"Why can't you just let me grow up!" Sugar Bag Baby had felt like shouting.

But Mum was already looking hurt. So he'd shut up. After all, there was one thing he felt really, truly grateful for. There was another photo upstairs. He was in his incubator. Looking like a scrawny, plucked chicken as usual. With a face the size of a ping-pong ball. But in this picture he was kicking his pipe-cleaner legs wide apart. And he had no nappy on.

"At least she didn't lend the fête that one!" Sugar Bag Baby muttered as he sat on the platform. The very thought of it as a huge, blow-up picture beside him made him writhe in horror.

But he didn't totally trust Mum. She'd do anything to raise money for premature babies. She was Big Chief on loads of committees. She'd made a career out of it! So, like he did every year at Fête-time, he'd hidden that photo under his mattress, just to make sure.

Whoops! He hadn't been paying attention. It would soon be time for him to be put on parade. Mrs Biggins was just finishing her speech.

"And, as I do every year, I'd like to remind you that our chosen charity is the premature baby unit at our local hospital. And here's living proof that your money really can make a difference! Our very own Sugar Bag Baby!"

"Why do they always call me that!" thought Sugar Bag Baby. He didn't mean, "Why do they call me Sugar Bag Baby". He'd got used to that. No one in the village ever called him anything else. What he was wondering was why they called him, "*Our* Sugar Bag Baby." Like everyone in the village owned a piece of him. "Like I'm public property!" thought Sugar Bag Baby as he shuffled forward.

"Without your generous gifts of money," said Mrs Biggins, "to pay for special medical equipment, Our Sugar Bag Baby might not be here today."

She ruffled his hair.

"Hey, get off me!" Sugar Bag Baby wanted to shout. "No-one's allowed to do that!" Except maybe his girlfriend. But how was he ever going to get a girlfriend, with a nickname like "Sugar Bag Baby?"

But, of course, he didn't shout out. Sugar Bag Baby felt guilty being rude or bad. What if someone who'd saved his life thought, "Look how he's turned out! Why did I give that two quid? It was money down the drain!"

Instead, he gave everyone a sickly smile. Which is a tough thing to do when you're gritting your teeth.

"I remember struggling from door to door with my collecting tin," Mrs Biggins told the crowd. "That snowy winter Our Sugar Bag Baby was born. It played havoc with my bad knee."

"Excuse me!" Sugar Bag Baby was

thinking. "But that's not exactly my fault. I didn't ask you to!"

"You selfish boy!" scolded a stern voice inside his head. "How can you be so ungrateful? She did her knee in so that you could LIVE!"

"But the pain was worth it," Mrs Biggins rambled on, "when I see what a lovely little lad he is now. He's a credit to us! Our own little ray of sunshine. Who, I'm sure, is grateful to the whole village for their generosity!"

Sugar Bag Bay curled his lip up again. It was supposed to be a smile. But it looked more like a wince of pain. "I am grateful!" he felt like shouting. "I am! I am. Honest!"

But how grateful can one kid be? To how many people. For how long? Was he never going to escape being their Sugar Bag Baby?

Mrs Biggins ruffled his hair again.

"AAAAARGH!" screamed Sugar Bag Baby inside his head while his face was smiling.

At last, he was allowed back to his seat. The little ray of sunshine sat hidden behind some bright balloons, scowling like a storm cloud.

"I wouldn't like to be that kid," said a voice.

"What?" thought Sugar Bag Baby. "Who said that?"

He twisted round. He looked down from the platform. There were two big boys right below him, sniggering about his photo. He could just see the tops of their shaved heads.

"Nah!" said the other. "I don't fancy his chances at our school. With a cissy name like Sugar Bag Baby! He won't last two minutes!"

"AAAAARGH!" Sugar Bag Baby gave another silent shriek. What school did they come from? They looked scary! Was it the Big School, the same one he was going to after the summer holidays?

He'd thought about it before, in a waffly sort of way. But those boys' sneery comments were the last straw. "You can't go out into the Big Wide World with a nickname like Sugar Bag Baby!" he decided. "You got to get rid of it once and for all."

Even then he dithered. It seemed like mission impossible.

Maybe, he tried to convince himself, when he got to Big School, his mates from his little village school would keep quiet about his nickname. He could start a whole new life!

"Dream on!" thought Sugar Bag Baby. The very first day, some teacher would say, "And what's your name?" And some blabber-mouth from his old

school would blurt out, "He's famous, Miss. He's Our Sugar Bag Baby!"

If there were any bullies listening in, their eyes would light up.

"They'll think it's their birthday!" thought Sugar Bag Baby.

His eyes grew steely with determination.

"It's TIME!" he told himself. "Time to break free! After I've finished, no one will call me Sugar Bag Baby ever again!"

CHAPTER TWO

Sugar Bag Baby's fight-back started next morning. He'd decided to be rude. Not just now and again. But ALL the time. For the rest of his life. That polite, smiling, grateful Sugar Bag Baby was gone for good.

"Like it's flushed down the toilet!" thought Sugar Bag Baby, joyfully. "Or blown up with a bomb!"

He experimented on Mum first. She asked him, "Do you want toast or cornflakes?"

"Whatever," said Sugar Bag Baby in a surly voice, shrugging. He didn't look her in the eye.

"Your big brother's passed all his school exams. He got the results this morning."

"So?" demanded Sugar Bag Baby. "How does that affect me exactly?"

"I just thought you'd be pleased for him," said Mum.

"Well, I'm not," scowled Sugar Bag Baby. "I couldn't care less. Right? I couldn't care less if he FAILED all of them! In fact, I'd be really happy!"

Mum gasped with horror. "What a terrible thing to say!"

When Sugar Bag Baby poured milk on his cornflakes, he made sure it slopped all over the table.

"You're being very unpleasant this morning," said Mum, sounding surprised. "Not like your usual self at all."

"Hey, that's great!" thought Sugar Bag Baby. "It's working already!"

But he knew Mum was a pushover. On account of him almost dying after he was born, she let him get away with all sorts. The real test was being rude in public.

"Mum thinks I just got out of bed on the wrong side," thought Sugar Bag

Baby, with a secret grin, as he slammed the back door. "She doesn't realise this is the new, rude ME!"

Outside in the street, he took a deep lungful of fresh air. He felt like a new person already!

"Whoops, nearly forgot!" He swapped the grin for a scowl and went slouching through the village.

He made himself swear a solemn promise. "The first person you meet, you've got to be really, really rude to them. All right?"

He giggled at the thought, "They're going to be dead shocked."

He heard someone hobbling up behind him. Here was his big chance! He screwed up his face into a ferocious sneer.

20

He felt someone ruffle his hair.

"AAAAARGH!" screamed Sugar Bag Baby inside his head.

It was Mrs Biggins. The woman who'd made herself lame so that he could live!

By the time Sugar Bag Baby turned round, there was a simpering smile on his face. "Hello, Mrs Biggins."

"Want a sweetie?" she said, taking a crumpled bag out of her cardie pocket.

"You were useless!" Sugar Bag Baby raged at himself after she'd gone. "You were really PATHETIC! You even took two of her pear drops and said, 'Thank you, Miss Biggins'!"

He was disgusted with himself. If he could, he'd have given himself a good kicking. "You should have said, right at the start, 'You stupid old wrinkly! Stop messing up my hair style!'"

But he'd chickened out! His very first attempt to be Rude Boy instead of Sugar Bag Baby had been a total flop. He tired to find excuses. "This being rude is too weedy, anyway. You need to do something much more radical!"

Then, out of the blue, he had the most brilliant idea.

Late that night, Mum saw a weird blue glow coming out from under Sugar Bag Baby's bedroom door. She yanked it open.

"You should be asleep!" she said. "Were you watching a video? I hope it wasn't one of your big brother's horror films!"

Sugar Bag Baby said nothing. But he looked guilty.

"What's it called?" demanded Mum. "*The Mad Axe Murderer* or something? Don't you dare put it on again. You'll give yourself nightmares!"

Sugar Bag Baby listened to Mum's footsteps clatter back down the stairs.

"Tee hee hee," he sniggered. "If she only knew what I'm really watching!"

It wasn't *The Mad Axe Murderer*. It was a video called, *How To Cut Your Hair*.

It had come free with Big Brother's electric head shaver. Sugar Bag Baby had borrowed that too.

"I'm gonna shave my head!" Sugar Bag Baby had told his big brother. "Like those two boys who made fun of me. Then I'll look tough. And no one will call me Sugar Bag Baby ever again!"

His plan had another major advantage. "And that Mrs Biggins won't be able to mess up my hair. 'Cos I won't have any!"

He was sure it would work. Once, they'd seen a boy his age in the street with a shaved head. And Mum had said, "He looks like a little thug!"

"Yeah! I want to look like a little thug!" Sugar Bag Baby had explained to his big brother.

Big Brother was hardly listening. But passing his exams had put him in a good mood. He gave Sugar Bag Baby some advice. "You'd better study that video," he said. "It's not as easy as it looks."

"I've done enough studying," thought Sugar Bag Baby. He was impatient to start. Secretly, in the dim light of his bedroom, he switched on the head shaver.

"Buzzzzz!" It sounded like an angry wasp.

He took a deep breath. He suddenly felt very nervous. He slid the shaver up the back of his neck. He did it again.

"Hey! This is easy peasy!" Pity he didn't have a mirror.

"AAAAARGH!" Sugar Bag Baby had just seen the hair, loads of it, drifting down onto his bedroom carpet. He dropped the head shaver, as if it was red hot. "What have I done?"

Big Brother came bursting in. "Did someone scream?"

"Am I bald?" asked Sugar Bag Baby, trembling. "What hair cut have I got? Is it a Mohican or something?"

"No, it's a Mushroom Cut," said Big Brother.

"A Mushroom Cut?" Sugar Bag Baby was horrified. "That's the silliest name for a haircut I ever heard! You're just making that up!"

"I'm not!" said Big Brother "I thought you'd done it deliberately. It's one of the haircuts on the video."

"But I wanted to look like a little thug!" wailed Sugar Bag Baby, wishing he'd watched that video the whole way through. "They wouldn't be seen dead with a Mushroom Cut!"

Then he calmed down. He'd found a crumb of comfort.

"At least no one will know it's a

Mushroom Cut but me. I mean, what other kid wants to watch a boring video called 'How To Cut Your Hair'?"

"Every kid in the village," said Big Brother. "Haven't you seen all the shaved heads around? I've been renting out that head shaver for ages. And I always tell 'em the same as I told you. Better study the video before you do it!"

"I don't believe this!" Sugar Bag Baby almost tore his hair out. But he didn't dare. He'd lost quite enough already. Mum was going to have a fit.

"By the way, you owe me two pounds," said Big Brother. "That's the charge for borrowing my head shaver."

"YOU MUST BE JOKING!" roared Sugar Bag Baby. He felt angry and sorry for himself at the same time. All his plans were wrecked!

Was Big Brother sniggering?

"Do you think this is funny?" bellowed Sugar Bag Baby. "You should try being me sometime. It was bad enough before, being Sugar Bag Baby. Now I'm Sugar Bag Baby with a Stupid Hair Style!"

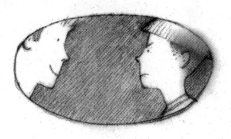

CHAPTER THREE

Sugar Bag Baby was heading round to his gran's for some comfort. When Mum saw his hair that morning she'd gone mad.

"What on earth did you think you were playing at?"

"He was trying to give himself a Mushroom Cut," explained Big Brother.

"No, I wasn't!"

But Mum had snipped away at it with scissors.

"That's better," she said, stroking

Sugar Bag Baby's head. "You look more like a fuzzy duckling now than a thug."

"AAAAARGH!" screamed Sugar Bag Baby, inside his head. What if he met one of his mates? And they shouted out, "Fuzzy Duckling!" He was sick of being Sugar Bag Baby. But he didn't want a nickname that was even cissier!

He took a secret route to Gran's so no-one could see him. Dodging down alley ways and sneaking from tree to tree like a spy.

But an old lady hanging out her washing, shouted out, "How's Our Sugar Bag Baby today?"

"Fine, thanks, Mrs Braithwaite!" Sugar Bag Baby shouted back before he could stop himself.

Sugar Bag Baby felt he always had to answer, "Fine!" Else people might say, "What's he looking so miserable for? Doesn't he know how lucky he is?

I gave my last one pee so he could LIVE!"

"Ow, ow, ow!" Sugar Bag Baby gave himself some hard thwacks on the forehead. He felt he deserved some punishment.

"What's the matter with you?" he raged at himself. "What did you say 'Fine' for? You're not supposed to be Sugar Bag Baby anymore!"

But who was he supposed to be instead? He didn't have a clue. Until he saw the newspaper lying on Gran's kitchen table.

He was munching his way through some breakfast cereal. Taking big handfuls straight out of the box. Gran's was a good place to come when you felt fed up. She let him eat whatever he liked. His mum would have asked him, like it was some kind of major crime, "Are you eating Chocolate-covered Wheaty Pops without milk?"

"Hey!" Sugar Bag Baby picked up the paper. He felt really excited. Suddenly, his plans to find himself a new image had come alive again.

"BALACLAVA BOY DEFIES POLICE!" shrieked the headline,

And there was a photo, of a boy in a black balaclava that covered his whole head. He looked really menacing. All you could see were his eyes and mouth. And the big pink tongue that he was sticking out at the world.

"Wow!" said Sugar Bag Baby. "Who's that?"

"You don't want to read about him," said Gran. "He's nothing but trouble. He's a really bad lad!"

"I'd like to be Balaclava Boy," said Sugar Bag Baby.

Gran was horrified. "You don't want to be him! He steals things from shops. Our Sugar Bag Baby would never steal anything!"

Sugar Bag Baby thought, "I'd better calm her down. She might have a heart attack."

"No, I don't actually want to be him," he explained quickly. "I just want to look like him, that's all."

Gran still seemed shocked and confused.

"I want a balaclava," said Suga Baby, trying to make her understand. It was that menacing look he was after. It was so sinister and scary. "If I looked like that," he thought, "no-one would call me Sugar Bag Baby ever again."

And, his plan had another big advantage he'd just thought of, a balaclava would hide this stupid hair cut!

To his amazement, Gran really did seem to understand. She was even eager to help him out. "Do you want a balaclava?" she said. She sounded pleased and surprised. "Wait until tomorrow, my pet," she told him. "And you shall have one!"

Sugar Bag Baby hurried back home. There was a new, hopeful spring in his step. Things were looking up.

"Mushroom Head!" said a kid's voice from behind a bush. It was obviously someone who'd watched the video all the way through.

But Sugar Bag Baby didn't care. By tomorrow, he wouldn't be Mushroom Head. He wouldn't be Sugar Bag Baby. He would be the fearsome Balaclava Boy.

The next day, Gran turned up, as promised. Sugar Bag Baby knew she would. Gran always kept her promises. She took a brown paper parcel out of her shopping bag.

Sugar Bag Baby was tingling all over with excitement. He could hardly wait. "In a few seconds," he was thinking. "There's gonna be a whole new ME!"

He snatched the parcel and ripped it open. He was already thinking, "Good riddance, Sugar Bag Baby!"

Then he saw what was inside.

"AAAAARGH!"

"That'll keep you nice and cosy," said Gran. "I knitted it myself."

"But Gran!"

Did Balaclava Boy's Gran knit his sinister headgear? "I don't think so!" thought Sugar Bag Baby. "And Gran, I wanted it black!"

"It is black!" said Gran. "I've just put some yellow stripes in it, that's all. To make it a bit more cheery."

"But I don't want it cheery," said Sugar Bag Baby, clenching his fists in frustration. "I want it scary!"

Gran didn't appreciate his problem. "Don't you like it, then?" she asked. She sounded upset. "I used to knit all your little bonnets when you were in that incubator."

"So it was you!" thought Sugar Bag Baby.

"Try it on," urged Gran.

Sugar Bag Baby was going to say, "No way!" but then Mum

walked in the room. "Go on! Your Gran spent hours knitting it. She missed her bingo."

Inside his head, Sugar Bag Baby was growling, "Grrrrrr!" But he was outnumbered. He dragged the balaclava over his head. He could hardly bear to look in the mirror.

"Oh no!" Gran hadn't lost the knack of knitting hats that made him look like a prat.

As well as being the wrong colour, it didn't have three little holes like Balaclava Boy's. It just had one big hole that his face poked through.

"I was supposed to look like Balaclava Boy!" roared Sugar Bag Baby. "But I look like a giant bee! I'm Bumble-bee Boy instead!"

Gran wasn't listening. She was rummaging in her bag for something else. "Actually," she said, "you know

those baby bonnets I knitted? Well, every one had its own pair of matching mittens! I had some wool left over. So I just thought you might like—"

"NO, NO, NO!" yelled Sugar Bag Baby, covering his ears.

"But..." said Gran, handing him a mitten-shaped parcel.

He couldn't stand it a second longer. He had to escape!

"I've got to go out! Right now!" yelled Sugar Bag Baby over his shoulder, as he grabbed his coat and dashed out of the front door.

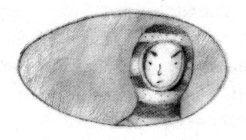

CHAPTER FOUR

"That's a nice tea cosy you're wearing," said a wheezy voice from somewhere behind Sugar Bag Baby.

"Aaargh!" Sugar Bag Baby ripped off Gran's balaclava. He'd raced out of the house so fast he'd forgotten he'd still got it on.

"Hello, Mr Robinson."

The wheezy voice belonged to the village's oldest inhabitant. Mr Robinson was 101. He had a neck like a wrinkly tortoise. But his little eyes were bright and wily. Every day, he sat on a seat near the bus stop with his scruffy old dog on a string. Both of them watched the world go by.

"You look like you've lost a shilling and found sixpence," said Mr Robinson to Sugar Bag Baby.

Sugar Bag Baby had hardly spoken ten words to Mr Robinson in his whole life. But today he just couldn't help blurting out his most secret feelings.

"I'm just fed up, that's all!"

"You're that Sugar Bag Baby, aren't you?" said Mr Robinson, peering at him. "What have you got to moan about?"

"See what I mean?" said Sugar Bag Baby "I'm not even allowed to be fed up! I hate being everybody's Sugar Bag Baby! I'm a big boy now! Or hasn't anyone noticed?"

"You're lucky," said Mr Robinson. "When I was your age, I was called Pink Slipper Cyril."

"Pardon?" said Sugar Bag Baby.

"I was born premature like you."

"Honest?" said Sugar Bag Baby. He was amazed. "I never knew that!"

"In those days there weren't all these fancy incubator things," Mr Robinson rambled on. "The doctor said, 'He's done for!' But my mum, she put me in one of her slippers to keep me warm."

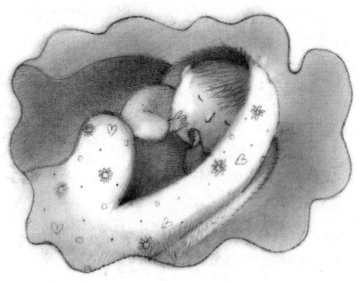

"You fitted inside your mum's slipper? You must have been minute," said Sugar Bag Baby.

"Not really," said Mr Robinson. "It's just that my Mum had enormous feet. Anyhow, the slipper was a pink one, see. And my first name is Cyril, so—"

"Yes, yes, I get it, " Sugar Bag Baby interrupted excitedly. "But the thing is, why doesn't anyone call you Pink Slipper Cyril now? How did you stop them doing it?"

Sugar Bag Baby waited eagerly for the reply. People said you should learn from the wisdom of old wrinklies. This could be the answer to all his problems!

Mr Robinson leaned closer. He had a bristly chin. His breath smelled of tobacco.

"I stopped them," he whispered, "by making sure that they're all dead."

"What?" said Sugar Bag Baby, backing away. "You mean you killed them all? Everyone who called you Pink Slipper Cyril?"

It sounded like an extreme solution. Was it really the only way to stop people calling you stupid nicknames?

"No, no, no!" frowned Mr Robinson. "I didn't kill them. I just made sure I lived longer than them, that's all. The last person who called me Pink Slipper Cyril died two years ago. He was ninety-nine. Now no-one round here remembers. I've outlived them all!"

Mr Robinson sounded really pleased about that.

But Sugar Bag Baby felt cheated.

"I can't wait that long!" he roared. Did he really have to reach 101 before people stopped calling him Sugar Bag Baby?

And what if it never happened? What if one of his mates lived to be 102?

"That would be just my luck!" thought Sugar Bag Baby.

He realised he was still clutching Gran's balaclava. He dropped it into the rubbish bin by the bus stop. "Good riddance!"

Then he stomped off, sunk in doom and gloom. Things looked blacker than ever. His mission to free himself from the name Sugar Bag Baby had been a dismal failure.

He gave some strict orders to his brain: "Remind me never to ask old people for their advice again!"

SPLASH!

Sugar Bag Baby was shocked out of his misery. The river was just behind those trees. And it sounded like someone had fallen in!

He went rushing to the bank. There were crazy dreams in his head. He could see the headlines now. "Young Hero in Riverbank Rescue." He could hear village people greeting him, "How's Our Young Hero today?" As a nickname, it knocked the spots off Sugar Bag Baby!

But when he saw who'd fallen in, his dreams burst like bubbles. It was his friend, Spud. He was thrashing about in the river, shouting, "Help! Help!"

But Sugar Bag Baby wasn't fooled. He could see the water was shallow where Spud was. Sugar Bag Baby felt desperately disappointed.

"Why did you get your hopes up?" he scolded himself.

He'd been watching too many cartoons on children's telly. Every week, those cartoon heroes got a chance to save the world. He was desperate to do his Superboy act. He didn't want to save the whole planet. He'd be happy with just one person.

"It's not fair," thought Sugar Bag Baby. "Why is no-one ever in trouble when I'm around?"

Just to make sure, he called out, hopefully, "You drowning, Spud?"

"Save me!" said Spud, as he stood up in the

water. It hardly reached his ankles. He staggered, dripping, up the bank. And shook himself all over Sugar Bag Baby like a wet dog.

Spud had a head shaped like a potato – that's how he got his nickname. Sugar Bag Baby envied him.

"He doesn't know how lucky he is," he'd often thought, "being called after a vegetable." He'd swap Sugar Bag Baby for Spud any day. Or for Carrot. Or even Turnip.

"I give up!" said Spud. "This is the third time I've fallen in. If you ask me, it's impossible!"

"What is?" asked Sugar Bag Baby.

"Getting across to the other bank without getting wet!"

"Spud, are you out of your mind? How can anyone do that?"

Spud pointed upwards. They were standing under a half-dead tree. Its branches snaked out in all directions. And dangling from one of them was a Tarzan swing made of twisted blue rope.

"I don't want to be Tarzi King anyway," said Spud, trudging off.

"Spud, wait!" shouted Sugar Bag Baby. "What do you mean, Tarzi King?"

Spud didn't stop. But he shouted, over his shoulder. "Us kids have decided. Whoever swings across first, gets to be called Tarzi King."

Sugar Bag Baby was startled by a sudden WHOOSH! of excitement inside him. Like a firework display, shooting out showers of golden stars.

"Tarzi King!" he said to himself. He tried out the nickname again. "Tarzi King."

"I could live with that," he decided. "It's good." It was better than good. Compared to Sugar Bag Baby, it was brilliant!

"I'm not trying again," was the last thing Spud shouted back before he squelched away. "What if I really did drown? My mum would kill me!"

Sugar Bag Baby was left all alone. The river rippled gently at the edges. But it was deep and swirling in the middle. Was it really that far to the other side? Sugar Bag Bay shivered. The sun was blazing down. So why did he feel this icy chill?

His stomach was fluttering too. As if someone had released a million butterflies inside it. The sensible part of his brain was telling him, "This is a very bad idea."

"Tell me a better one then!" snapped Sugar Bag Baby. "Or shut up!"

Sugar Bag Baby grasped the rope. He walked backwards with it. Then he took a running jump.

"AHHHH-A-AHHHH-A-AHHHH!" With a wild Tarzan cry, he swooped through space. Trees and water rushed by in a blue-green blur. The rope whisked away, out of his hands. But Sugar Bag Baby flew on. Whump! He slammed into something hard. For a while, he lay there, winded.

"Where am I?" thought Sugar Bag Baby. He got shakily to his feet. He saw the half-dead tree. He saw the blue rope dangling down. They were

both on the opposite bank of the river.

"I did it!" thought Sugar Bag Baby, thrilled to bits. "I'm on the other side!"

His hands were red with rope burns. He felt black and blue with bruises. But who cared about that?

"Yay!" He punched his fist in the air. He was really proud of himself. "I am Tarzi King now! Bye Bye, Sugar Bag Baby."

He felt free at last. He felt fresh and new. Like a snake that's burst out of its tight old skin.

Then he had a shattering thought. "Nobody saw me!" If he told his mates, 'I made it across the river,' they'd say straightaway, 'Prove it.'

"Doh!" Sugar Bag Baby crumpled back onto the bank. He thwacked himself hard on the forehead. "You stupid fool!" he raged at himself. "You should have set this up better! You should have asked Spud to stay."

Then he heard rustling in the long grass. Was Spud still hanging around? Sugar Bag Baby leapt to his feet. "Hey, Spud!" he shouted. "Did you see what I just did? I went flying across that river! How brave was that?"

"It wasn't brave at all. It was very dangerous!" a voice answered.

"Oh no," thought Sugar Bag Baby "Mrs Biggins!"

He was in deep trouble now. Instead of getting a pat on the back, he was in for a big telling-off.

She came puffing up, "You nearly scared me to death!"

He could guess what she was going to say, "Our Sugar Bag Baby shouldn't risk his life like that! How selfish! When we all worked so hard to save you!"

"I'm gonna tell her it's my life!" muttered Sugar Bag Baby. "And she can get lost!"

But another voice inside his head argued, "You did her knee in. You nearly scared her to death. You can't be rude to her as well!"

"Hello, Mrs Biggins," he said. "Sorry about the scare."

Mrs Biggins started off, "What would we do if anything happened to Our Sugar Bag Baby?"

"Here we go," thought Sugar Bag Baby, gritting his teeth.

"When you were born, it was the best thing that happened to our village."

"Pardon?" said Sugar Bag Baby.

"They were bad times then," said Mrs Biggins, shaking her head, grimly. "It was the worst winter in ages. The carpet factory had just closed. Half the village was out of work. When you lived it gave us all something to celebrate. You were our light in the darkness. Our little miracle!"

If Mrs Biggins thought what she'd said would make Sugar Bag Baby feel better, she was wrong.

"I'm not your little miracle!" screamed Sugar Bag Baby, inside his head. "I'm just ME. An ORDINARY BOY!"

Mrs Biggins ruffled his Mushroom Cut. "What's happened to your hair?" she said. "You feel like a lovely fuzzy duckling."

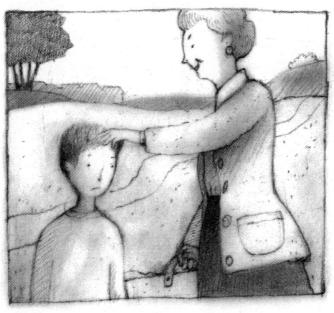

Sugar Bag Baby waited until she'd gone.

Then he opened his mouth wide. "AAAAAAAAAARGH!"

His cry of despair echoed right down the river. Two swans took off and went clattering away over the trees.```

CHAPTER FIVE

Sugar Bag Baby went stomping down to the village Mini-Mart. His face was stormy. It was time to do something really drastic.

Being a bad lad would stop people calling him Sugar Bag Baby. He'd already worked that one out. "It's just that you haven't been bad enough yet!" he told himself.

But, this time, he was going to shock everyone. The whole village would say, "He's really let us all down!"

"Good!" thought Sugar Bag Baby, grimly. "They won't want me for their Sugar Bag Baby any more. Not after what I'm going to do!"

The village shop was busy. Plenty of witnesses. That was just what he needed.

He hung about by the chocolate bars. He was scared. His stomach felt scrunched up, small as a walnut. "Do you really want to do this?"

said that voice in his head.

Sugar Bag Baby hesitated. Then he remembered those sneering boys at the Fund Raising Fête. "He won't last two minutes at our school."

"I've got no other choice!" thought Sugar Bag Baby, in a panic.

He snatched the biggest chocolate bar off the shelf. He walked straight past the checkout lady. She didn't shout, "Hey! Wait!"

"What's the matter with her?" thought Sugar Bag Baby. "Is she blind or what?" He wasn't even trying to hide the bar. He'd practically waved it under her nose!

"Didn't you see?" said Sugar Bag Baby, going back. "I was walking right out of the shop. With this chocolate bar I haven't paid for."

"I saw!" smiled the lady on the till. "But I wasn't worried. I knew Our Sugar Bag Baby would never steal.

I knew you'd come back to pay for it. And I was right, wasn't I? That's ninety pence, please."

As he dug in his pocket for the cash, Sugar Bag Baby was silently screaming inside his head.

"You're useless!" he scolded himself, savagely. "All your plans have gone wrong! You can't even get yourself arrested!"

He had one last desperate try. "But I'm a criminal!" he told the check-out lady. "Like that Balaclava Boy. Call the police! I should be locked up!"

But the checkout lady wasn't even listening. She was too busy talking to the lady behind him. They seemed very excited about something. "They're already collecting for him," she was saying. "He needs very special care. Look, his picture's on the front cover."

"Awwwww!" said the other lady, picking up the local paper from the counter. "Isn't he cute?"

Sugar Bag Baby looked at the photo. He felt suddenly sick and dizzy.

"It's me!" he thought, horrified. "Me, in the hospital!"

It was that same squirm-making picture. The one where he looked like a naked mole rat, wearing frilly bootees and a fluffy wool bonnet, knitted by Gran.

"Mum wouldn't have! She couldn't have!" his brain shrieked at him.

Hadn't Mum used him enough for her fundraising campaigns? Surely she hadn't made them splash his baby photos all over the paper again?

But when he read the head line, it didn't mention Sugar Bag Baby.

"TEA CUP KID SURVIVES AGAINST ALL THE ODDS," it said.

"Doh?" thought Sugar Bag Baby. "What's all that about then?"

The checkout lady was eager to tell him. "A baby's been born in the village," she said. "And he's small enough to sit in a tea cup. The papers are already calling him the Tea Cup Kid."

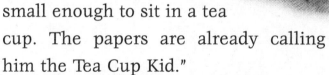

"Yes and he's much smaller than you when you were born," said another woman.

Sugar Bag Baby didn't like her tone. It sounded a bit spiteful. As if she was saying, 'The Tea Cup Kid is much more famous than you!'

"Here's your change, Christopher," said the checkout lady.

Sugar Bag Baby nearly fell over backwards. At first he looked round and thought, "Christopher? Who's this guy, Christopher?" Then he thought he hadn't heard right.

But the checkout lady said, "Christopher? Do you want this change or not?"

"She called me Christopher!" he thought, amazed. It was his real name.

No-one in the village had called him Christopher for ages.

He should be celebrating. He should be turning cartwheels, setting off fireworks. Punching the air and yelling, "Free at last!"

The Tea Cup Kid had saved him. He'd come along just in time and pushed him into second place. Everyone was talking about the new star. Soon people would forget that there'd ever been a Sugar Bag Baby.

"It's just what you've always wanted," Christopher told himself. "To be an ordinary boy! You should be dancing in the street! You should be going bananas!"

So why did he feel some regrets as well? He thought of all the fuss people made of him, "How's our Sugar Bag Baby today?" He thought of Mrs Biggins saying, "You were our light in the darkness." A kid couldn't help getting a warm glow when he was called that.

He shook himself, hard. "That's over!" he told himself. "You're Christopher now. Not Sugar Bag Baby!"

He looked again at the photo of the Tea Cup Kid. He wasn't a pretty sight, either. He looked like a big white maggot with a bonnet on.

"I feel sorry for that Tea Cup Kid," thought Christopher. For a start, he was stuck with an even sillier nickname.

"You don't know what you're in for," he told the photo of Tea Cup Kid, "when you take over from me. No one will ever call you by your real name. People will always say, 'You should be grateful!' And your mum will save that picture to show to your girlfriend."

But then he had a comforting idea.

"You'll always have a friend," he

promised Tea Cup Kid. "A friend who knows just what you feel like. Because they've been through it!"

Just saying that made him feel immediately older and wiser. As if he'd grown up in one giant leap.

"Yes," Christopher decided, "me and that Tea Cup Kid will stick together. I'll be like his big brother. He's going to have a lot to put up with."

Unless, of course, one day, Egg Cup Kid was born and pushed him into second place.

Look out for more Green Apples from
ORCHARD BOOKS...

JALOPY

GERALDINE McCAUGHREAN
Illustrated by Ross Collins

JALOPY

BY GERALDINE McCAUGHREAN

Masher and Spug ran out of the bank, chased by ten security guards, two big dogs and the clang of alarm bells. "Quick! Into the car!" cried Masher. But Jalopy was gone.

Mrs Ethel Thomas wins a beautiful shiny red car in a competition and calls the car Jalopy. But Mrs Thomas can't drive, so the car goes nowhere until one day bank-robbers Spug and Masher steal Jalopy to be their get-away car...

An exciting and funny story by a much-loved author.

MONKEY-MAN

SANDRA GLOVER

Illustrated by Garry Parsons

BY SANDRA GLOVER

"It was like a Yeti or giant ape covered in long, black hair. With huge, mad, glinting eyes. About seven feet tall. Wearing nothing but a pair of baggy shorts!"

There's a hairy, scary werewolf terrorising the neighbourhood! Max and his sister, Kerry, know the creature's *real* secret. But saving the day may turn out to be a closer shave than they had anticipated...

A hilarious story from an acclaimed author.

THE UGLY
GREAT GIANT

MALACHY DOYLE
Illustrated by David Lucas

THE UGLY GREAT GIANT

BY MALACHY DOYLE

"But I've won your land and I've won your cattle. What else is there to play for?" asked Sam.

"Oh, I can think of something," said the giant with an even uglier look than before... "Your head!"

When the Ugly Great Giant challenges Sam to a game of cards, there's a lot at stake. If Sam's going to outwit the foul and horrible monster, he's going to have to think fast!

A contemporary fairytale, told with style and originality, from an award-winning author.

ORCHARD GREEN APPLES

HARDBACK

☐ Monkey-Man   *Sandra Glover*   1 84362 276 9

☐ The Ugly Great Giant *Malachy Doyle*   1 84362 240 8

☐ Jalopy   *Geraldine McCaughrean* 1 84362 266 1

☐ Sugar Bag Baby   *Susan Gates*   1 84362 070 7

ALL PRICED AT £8.99

PAPERBACK

☐ Monkey-Man   *Sandra Glover*   1 84362 278 5

☐ The Ugly Great Giant *Malachy Doyle*   1 84362 241 6

☐ Jalopy   *Geraldine McCaughrean* 1 84362 267 X

☐ Sugar Bag Baby   *Susan Gates*   1 84362 071 5

ALL PRICED AT £3.99

Orchard Green Apples are available from all good bookshops,
or can be ordered direct from the publisher:
Orchard Books, PO BOX 29, Douglas IM99 1BQ
Credit card orders: please telephone 01624 836000 or fax 01624 837033
or visit our Internet site: www.wattspub.co.uk
or e-mail: bookshop@enterprise.net for details.

To order please quote title, author and ISBN
and your full name and address.
Cheques and postal orders should be made payable to 'Bookpost plc.'
Postage and packing is FREE within the UK
(overseas customers should add £1.00 per book).
Prices and availability are subject to change.